TOO COOL

Cricket Legend

Phil Kettle
illustrated by Craig Smith

SCHOLASTIC
SYDNEY AUCKLAND NEW YORK TORONTO LONDON
MEXICO CITY NEW DELHI HONG KONG

LEXILE™ 420

Scholastic Education
345 Pacific Highway
Lindfield NSW 2070
an imprint of Scholastic Australia Pty Limited (ABN 11 000 614 577)
PO Box 579, Gosford NSW 2250.
www.scholastic.com.au
www.toocoolrules.com

Part of the Scholastic Group
Sydney ● Auckland ● New York ● Toronto ● London ● Mexico City
● New Delhi ● Hong Kong

First published by Scholastic Education in 2001.
Text copyright © Phillip Kettle, 2001.
Illustrations copyright © black dog books and Springhill Pty Ltd, 2001.

a black dog and Springhill book

National Library of Australia Cataloguing-in-Publication entry
Kettle, Phillip, 1955-
    Toocool, Cricket Legend.
    ISBN 1 86504 335 4.
    1. Cricket - Juvenile fiction. I. Smith, Craig, 1955-.
    II. Title. (Series: Toocool).
A823.4

Typeset in Plantin.
Printed by McPherson's Printing Group, Maryborough Vic.

10 9 8 7 6 5 4 3 2   1 2 3 4 5 / 0

Contents

Marcy

Marcy's sister

Toocool

Dog

Chapter 1
Being Bored

I bowled the perfect leg break—straight down the hall. It had flight and drift. But when the ball hit the carpet, it turned the wrong way. It didn't take the off stump as I planned. Instead, it shot into the kitchen. Crash!

The vase on the kitchen table hit the floor.

"Toocool! I told you not to play cricket inside!" Mum shouted. "That vase was ninety years old."

Well, if it was that old, why was Mum worried about it getting broken?

I went back to the change room. I pinned a picture of the Australian Cricket Team on the board. They were going to be a lot better this season—now that I was captain.

I found my batting gloves at the bottom of the cupboard and put them on. I grabbed my bat and stood in front of the long mirror. I practised my straight drives, square cuts and hooks. If the English team could see me now, they would run all the way home.

Mum poked her head in the change room door.

"Toocool. You're going to Marcy's for the day. I have to go to work."

"But Mum, Marcy won't know a thing about cricket. And she doesn't even have a backyard. I'll be so bored."

"Maybe you can listen to the game on the radio," Mum said. She shut the door.

It was going to be a long, boring day. I whistled to Dog. At least he would be with me.

Chapter 2
The Pitch Report

Mum rang the doorbell. Marcy answered—she was wearing cricket pads. Her big sister was beside her.

"We're going to the park," Marcy said. "Hope you brought your cricket gear."

I ran back to the car. Things were looking up.

"I'm captain of England,"
Marcy said, as we walked to
the park. "They need all the
help they can get."

That suits me, I thought.
Only a legend could save
England, and I was the only
legend in this street.

The ground staff had prepared the oval well. It only needed finishing touches. Marcy banged the stumps into the ground. Then she marked out the pitch with a piece of chalk. All that was left was the pitch report. That was a job for an expert, so I did it.

"Greetings, viewers. Welcome to the world's greatest cricket ground. It's a wonderful day. People have come in their thousands to watch this battle.

Now for the key test. Yes, the key sticks into the ground easily. A perfect pitch. We're in for a great game."

Chapter 3
A Few **Surprises**

As usual, I won the toss.
I decided to put England in to
bat first. The English captain
looked worried. I didn't blame
her. I was the fastest bowler
ever to come out of Australia.

My run-up was marked on
the ground. I turned and waved
to the crowd. The chant went
up, "Come on, Toocool, come
on."

I rubbed the ball hard on
my leg. I wanted to give it as
much shine as I could.
I wanted it to swing.

I stood at my bowling mark.
I looked at Marcy. I was sure
I could see her shaking.

My run-up was as smooth
as silk. My speed increased
with every stride. When
I finally let the ball go, it
left my hand like a missile.
No way Marcy could hit that.

Whack! The ball flew straight back at me and over my head. It sailed through the sky and hit the fence. Marcy had hit a four!

Beginner's luck, for sure.

Next ball I definitely had
Marcy out. It had to be LBW.
But there was a loud appeal.
We asked Marcy's sister to
umpire. But, no matter what
I said, she would not say it was
out—I think she was on
England's side too.

But my fans were behind me
all the way. They had never
seen anyone bowl as fast as
Toocool.

In the third over, my luck
changed. Marcy played her first
shot back down the pitch. As
quick as a flash, Dog was on it.
He sprinted back with the ball.
There was no chance of
England getting a run when
Dog kept his eye on the ball.

I wiped my brow with my sleeve. I polished the ball. I got ready to bowl my famous leg spinner.

I turned to face the batter. But the crowd was going crazy. There was a pitch invasion. Two poodles, a terrier and Dog.

I yelled at Dog to get back.
I tried hard to ignore the fuss.
I didn't want my concentration
broken. All my focus was on
bowling England out. It was
time for the world's leading spin
bowler to strut his stuff—and
everybody knew his name,
"Toocool! Toocool!"

Chapter 4
Dog—the Traitor

All eyes were on me as I came in to bowl my first leg spinner. The ball left my hand and shot down the leg side. Marcy decided not to play it!
She just stood there and let it go past. What a major mistake for England!

The ball hit the pitch.
Then it turned and ripped
the off stump straight out of
the ground!

The crowd went wild. I took
a Toocool bow. I knew that
history would judge that as the
best ball ever bowled in Test
Cricket.

I was really firing—until
England announced it was time
to break for lunch.

After lunch, it was time for Toocool to face the might of the English bowlers. I walked to the centre wicket. The crowd became silent. I looked around at the field. England had Dog fielding for them. Dog was a full-time fielder. He never got to bat.

Marcy moved in to bowl.
It was a short ball. It had
plenty of bounce. I stood
straight and hooked the ball.
It headed for the fence. It had
to be a four. But Dog had
other ideas.

He pounced on the ball just before it reached the boundary. Then he raced it back to Marcy.

Dog, the traitor, was playing well for England.

Chapter 5
The Fatal Six

By the third over, I was scoring runs freely. I was a true all-rounder—a great bowler and a great batter.

I felt sure that a century was not far off. I think I only needed about ten more runs. But then I hit the fatal six.

The ball cleared the fence by a mile. Then it rolled into the gutter and disappeared. We searched for ages but we never found it. Our ball had been washed away.

Marcy declared the game a draw—but I didn't think the scores were that close. She was just nervous because England was losing. We all knew Australia would have won—if only I had found the ball and completed my century.

Oh well. It was only the first Test.

And besides, the Great Kart race was coming up. I might want Marcy on my side...

The End!

Toocool's
Cricket Glossary

Leg break—This is a ball that is bowled out of the back of the bowler's hand. When it lands, it turns away from a right-handed batter.

Leg side—If you are a right-handed batter and the ball comes down your left side, the ball has been bowled down the leg side.

Leg spinner—A bowler who bowls leg breaks.

Off stump—If the batter is right-handed, then the off stump is the stump that is on the right side of the batter.

Toocool's Backyard
The Cricket Ground

Marcys' place (England)

→ →
↓
→

Grandstand

The Gabba
Pitch
in
T.C. Park

Grandstand

The direction my six was travelling... the direction my six was lost forever...

← The Deli
(where we got an icecream) after.

Toocool's Quick Summary
of the game called cricket

Cricket is played by two teams. Each team has 11 players. The teams take turns batting and bowling. They play on an oval with a cricket pitch in the middle.

A cricket pitch is the shape of a rectangle. At each end of the pitch there are three sticks stuck in the ground. These are the stumps and together with the bails, they form the wickets.

Bowlers try to hit the stumps with the ball to get the batter out. But the batter tries to hit the ball first.

When you hit the ball, you can run really fast from one end of the pitch to the other. That's how you score runs. Other times you don't have to run. If you hit the ball over the fence, you get six runs without even running!

Batting is risky business. You can be bowled out, run out, caught out or stumped.

At the end of the game the team with the most runs wins.

The **Cricket** Ground

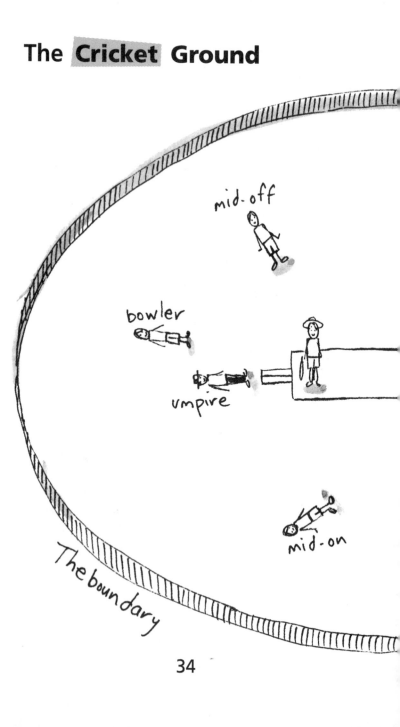

mid-off

bowler

umpire

mid-on

The boundary

34

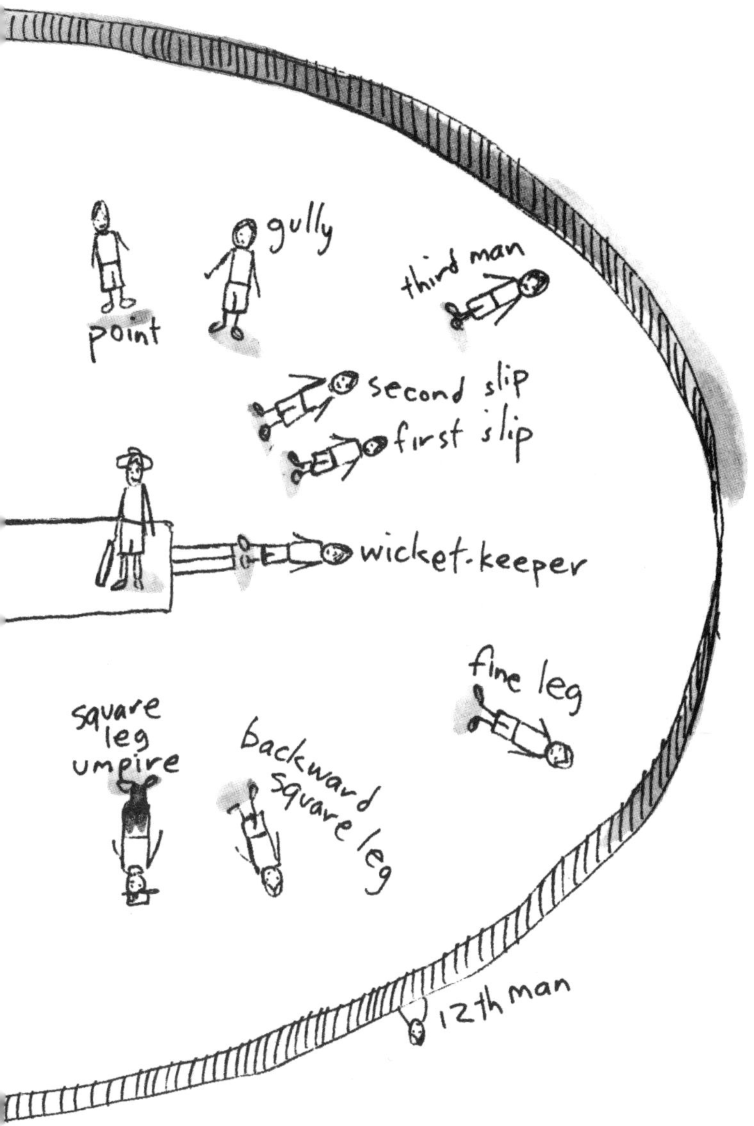

point

gully

third man

second slip

first slip

wicket-keeper

fine leg

square leg umpire

backward square leg

12th man

Q & A with Toocool—
he answers his own questions

Why do you think you were chosen to captain the Australian Cricket Team?

I'm a natural leader. I know a lot about getting the best out of a team. That's important when you're a captain. The team must respect you. I'm also a talented all-rounder.

What is an all-rounder?

An all-rounder is good at everything. I'm an all-rounder because I'm such a great bowler, a record-breaking batter and an excellent fielder.

 What is a century?

A century is when you score one hundred runs without getting out. I have scored several centuries. That's why the crowd love me so much. They love to see a batter score a century.

Do you like batting more than bowling?

I love batting because it keeps the crowd happy. But bowling is my favourite. I can bowl everything.

I can bowl leg spinners, off breaks, inswingers and outswingers. And every batter is terrified that I will bowl them a bouncer.

How long have you been playing cricket?

I have been playing cricket since I started walking. When I was a little kid I had a plastic bat and ball. It was useless. I used a piece of wood and a tennis ball instead.

I finally got a real cricket set when I was about six. It had pads and gloves, as well as two sets of stumps.

Where do you play?

I play in the backyard, at school, at the park and at the beach.

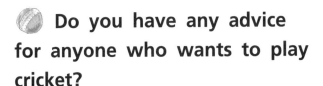 **Do you have any advice for anyone who wants to play cricket?**

Yes. Wear a hat and lots of sunscreen. And make sure you yell "HOWZAT" whenever you think someone is out. And never, ever go out for a duck.

 What's a duck?

It's when you get out without scoring any runs. I've been told it's terrible.

Cricket Quiz
How much do you know about cricket?

Q1 How many players are there in a cricket team?
A. 10. *B.* 7. *C.* 11.

Q2 How many umpires are there in a game of cricket?
A. 2. *B.* 1. *C.* Everyone in the crowd is an umpire.

Q3 If Toocool hits the ball over the fence, how many runs does he score?
A. 2. *B.* 4. *C.* 6.

Q4 Toocool hits the ball. The fielder catches it, but drops it. Is Toocool out?

A. Yes. *B.* No! *C.* It depends who is umpiring.

Q5 If you bowl a wide ball, what has happened?

A. The ball is out of shape.
B. The ball is too far out for the batter to hit. *C.* You've bowled a basketball instead of a cricket ball.

Q6 What does it mean if the umpire points up at the sky?

A. The batter is out.
B. There is a plane going over.
C. The umpire has a question.

Q7 What does the wicket-keeper do?

A. Keeps wickets. *B.* Stands behind the wicket and catches the balls the batter misses. *C.* Keeps score.

Q8 How many runs make a century?

A. 10. *B.* 80. *C.* 100.

Q9 When do you shout "HOWZAT"?

A. When someone is cheating. *B.* When you think someone is out. *C.* If you are cheering in Russian.

Q10 What does LBW stand for?
A. Left behind wicket. *B.* Leg before wicket. *C.* Last ball wins.

ANSWERS

1 C. **2** A. **3** C.
4 B. **5** B. **6** A.
7 B. **8** C. **9** B.
10 B.

If you got ten questions right, the cricket world wants you. If you got more than five right, you're showing promise. If you got less than five right, take up lawn bowls.

TooCool

Kart Master

Every kid on the block
has signed up for the
Great Kart race. But
there can only be one
winner...

Other titles in the **Toocool** series:

Toocool Tennis Ace
Toocool Footy Hero
Toocool Slam Dunk Magician
Toocool Grand Prix Champ
Toocool Fishing Fanatic
Toocool Surfing Pro